ALIEN INVADERS

Don't miss any of the titles

in the ALIEN INVADERS series:

ROCKHEAD: THE LIVING MOUNTAIN

INFERNOX: THE FIRESTARTER

ZILLAH: THE FANGED PREDATOR

HYDRONIX: DESTROYER OF THE DEEP

ATOMIC: THE RADIOACTIVE BOMB

KRUSH: THE IRON GIANT

JUNKJET: THE FLYING MENACE

MINOX: THE PLANET DRILLER

ZIPZAP: THE REBEL RACER

TANKA: THE BALLISTIC BLASTER

ALIEN INVAD' ZIPZAP, THE REBEL RACER
A RED FOX BOOK 978 1 849 41237 7

First published in Great Britain by Red Fox,
an imprint of Random House Children's Publisher's UK
A Random House Group Company

This edition published 2012

1 3 5 7 9 10 8 6 4 2

The Random House Group Limited supports the Forest Stewardship
Council (FSC®), the leading international forest certification organization.
Our books carrying the FSC label are printed on FSC®-certified paper.
FSC is the only forest certification scheme endorsed by the leading
environmental organizations, including Greenpeace. Our paper
procurement policy can be found at www.randomhouse.co.uk/environment

Set in Century Schoolbook

Red Fox Books are published by
Random House Children's Publisher's UK,
61–63 Uxbridge Road, London W5 5SA

www.**randomhousechildrens**.co.uk
www.**randomhouse**.co.uk

Addresses for companies within The Random House Group Limited can be
found at: www.randomhouse.co.uk/offices.htm

THE RANDOM HOUSE GROUP Limited Reg. No. 954009

A CIP catalogue record for this book is available from
the British Library.

Printed and bound in Great Britain by
CPI Group (UK) Ltd, Croydon, CR0 4YY

ALIEN INVADERS

MAX SILVER

ZIPZAP
THE REBEL RACER

RED FOX

THE GALAXY

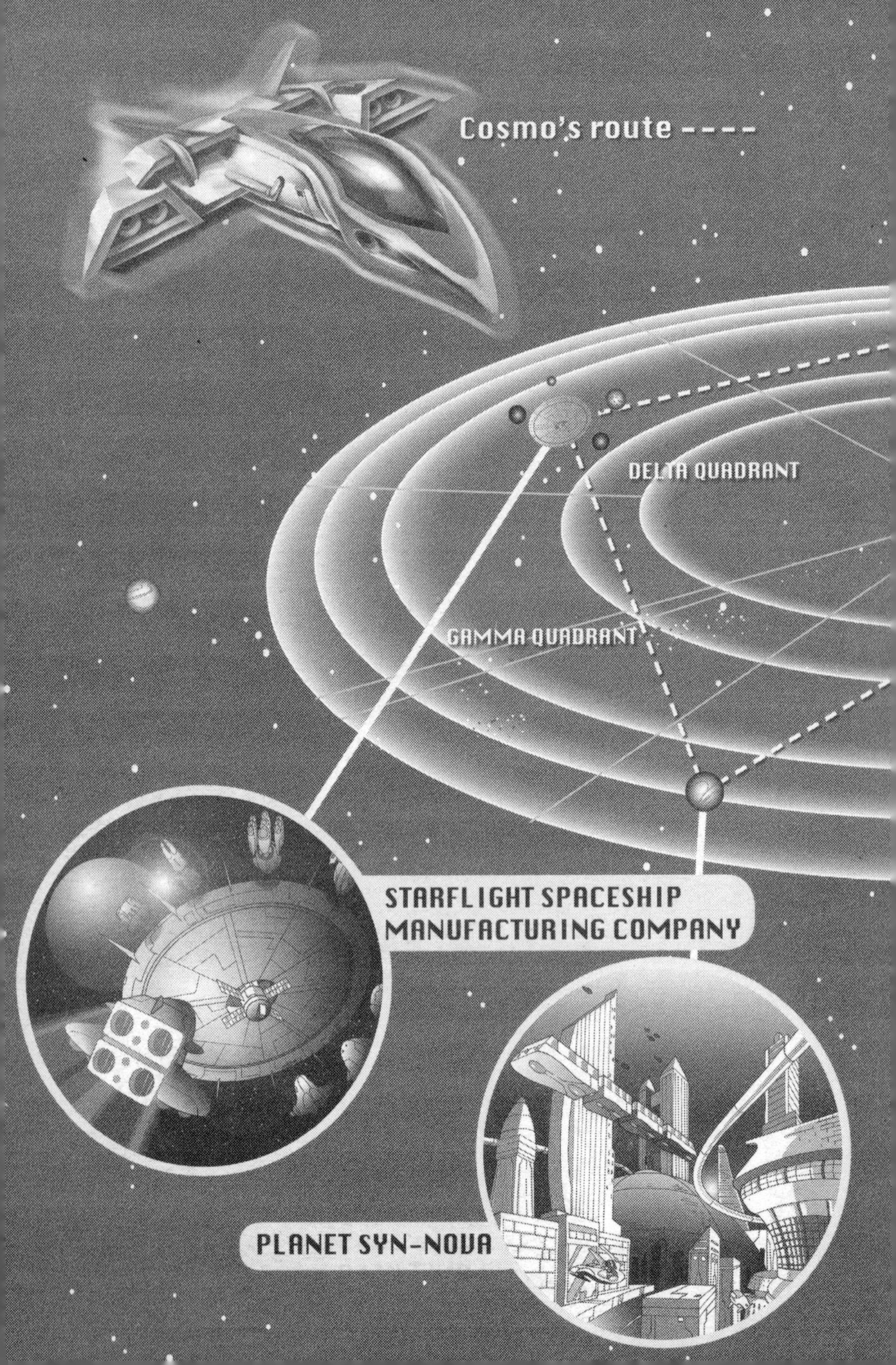

Cosmo's route - - - -

DELTA QUADRANT

GAMMA QUADRANT

STARFLIGHT SPACESHIP MANUFACTURING COMPANY

PLANET SYN-NOVA

PLANET BALAZ

SYSTEM OPEX
ALPHA QUADRANT
MOON OF GARR
GALACTIC CORE
BETA QUADRANT
THE WRECKING ZONE
PLANET KEFU

RESISTANCE IS FUTILE, EARTHLINGS!

MY NAME IS KAOS, AND MY WAR WITH YOUR GALAXY IS ENTERING A NEW PHASE...

THE YEAR IS 2121 AND I HAVE JOINED FORCES WITH METALLICON ALIENS FROM THE UNIVERSE'S WRECKING ZONE. THEY HAVE THE POWER OF LIVING MACHINES, AND I AM PROGRAMMING THEM TO INVADE YOUR GALAXY.

YOUR SECURITY FORCE, G-WATCH, WILL BE POWERLESS TO DEFEND YOU, AND ITS EARTHLING AGENT, COSMO SANTOS, WILL BE ANNIHILATED ALONG WITH HIS FRIENDS.

RESISTANCE IS FUTILE, EARTHLINGS. THE GALAXY WILL BE MINE!

INVADER ALERT!

As dawn broke over System Opex, Galactovision's holographic sports commentator, Rocco Wang, stepped among the line-up of rally vehicles at the start of the 207th Rawbone Rally. He faced a tiny hovering camera, his digital body flickering. "Thanks for tuning in, folks! The suns of Opex are rising and the drivers are ready to go. Welcome to the toughest land race in the galaxy!"

The light from Opex's first and smallest sun cast a red glow over the vehicles as they revved their engines: X-trucks, skidrons, armoured carts, roadsters, firebikes, dirt racers; their rugged riders the very best from the galactic sport of extreme rally racing. Galactovision's flying-eye cameras, called galactocams, zipped through the air on tiny wings, beaming images live to the people of the galaxy.

"In pole position is the reigning champ, Axel Crock!" Rocco exclaimed, edging to a chain-wheeler at the front of the grid driven by a bull-horned man. "Hey, Axel, do you think you can win again and beat your rivals, Zimla Cordosa and Ji-Phon?"

Axel Crock coolly revved the chain-wheeler's engine and exhaust smoke billowed around Rocco.

"I'll take that as a *yes*," the commentator smiled, fanning the air with his holographic hands.

Rocco Wang was well known to racing fans: a lifelike hologram in a purple space suit who had commentated on every Rawbone Rally in living memory, his digital body unaffected by the 800 kilometres of hostile planetary conditions that the racers had to contend with.

He glanced up excitedly as the second sun of Opex rose above the horizon, signalling the start of the race. With a roar of engines and a screech of tyres, the rally cars accelerated from the starting grid, dust and exhaust fumes filling the air. Rocco dashed to the sidelines among the emergency support vehicles. "They're off, folks! The 207th Rawbone Rally is underway!"

The rally cars sped towards the Moving Mountains of Antram. As the mountains shifted, gorges opened and closed between them, providing temporary routes through for the fastest drivers. The racers jostled for position, pursued by galactocams.

Rocco Wang shouted above the noise: "The drivers will have to brave moving mountains, ice blizzards, scorching deserts and even active volcanoes. First to the Pillars of Rawbone wins." A wild storm rumbled overhead. "The conditions are *fierce* today, folks!"

Suddenly there came an almighty thunderclap and the sky flashed as something like a lightning bolt landed among the racers, gouging a large crater in the ground. Rally cars swerved to avoid it, crashing into each other and flipping over, tyres and metal flying off.

"Jeepers! What was *that*?" Rocco yelled, hurrying to the scene of the crash. His holographic body flickered with electrostatic interference, then warped as a huge machine-like creature rose from the crater on a single spinning wheel.

"*Whoa!* Who's *that* guy?" Rocco exclaimed.

The machine-like alien sparked with electricity. Bolts of lightning shot from his metal hands blasting passing rally cars. "I am Zipzap," he roared, "and I will FRY you all!"

CHAPTER ONE

SYSTEM OPEX

Cosmo pulled back the throttle of the Dragster 7000 spaceship, blasting through the galaxy's Alpha Quadrant. "Awesome, we're going to the Rawbone Rally!" he said excitedly to his Etrusian co-pilot, Agent Nuri. "I've watched it loads of times on Galactovision."

"Me too," Nuri replied, looking up from the navigation console. "The racers are cool! Zimla Cordosa's my favourite."

From the control desk, the ship's brainbot, Brain-E, bleeped anxiously. "The rally will already be underway," it said. "I do hope the racers are OK."

Cosmo frowned, remembering he was going to the Rawbone Rally not as a sports fan, but as a G-Watch agent on a mission. "Brain-E, see if you can tune into Galactovision for the latest rally news. Let's hope nothing bad has happened."

The brainbot began searching the frequencies on the ship's communications console as Cosmo powered the Dragster onwards through the galaxy.

He was on a mission for the security force, G-Watch, to save the galaxy from five fearsome alien invaders – metallicons from a distant spacedump known as the Wrecking Zone, being beamed in by the outlaw Kaos. So far Cosmo had defeated three of them:

Krush, the iron giant; Junkjet, the flying menace; and Minox, the planet driller. Now he was heading after the fourth, Zipzap, spotted by G-Watch's scanners beaming towards System Opex, home of the famous Rawbone Rally.

"What's up with the signal, Brain-E?" Cosmo asked, seeing fuzzy video images flickering on the ship's monitor.

"Galactovision's transmission appears to be having some kind of problem," Brain-E replied.

"That's not a good sign," Cosmo said, glancing nervously at Nuri.

"Approaching System Opex now," she said. She tapped the Dragster's spacescreen, activating its star plotter, and words lit up on the glass, labelling the astral objects in view: COMET RAPTOR, NEWTON'S NEBULA, the twin stars ECHELA and ECHELO, and, in the distance, an enormous, irregular-shaped celestial

body marked SYSTEM OPEX. The strange mass had been formed centuries earlier when a solar system imploded and its planets collided with one another to create a single huge mass of shifting landscapes and climates. It was the perfect environment for the toughest all-terrain land rally in the galaxy.

Brain-E bleeped from the communications console. "The signal's

coming through now, Master Cosmo."

As Cosmo powered the Dragster between the twin stars Echela and Echelo, a video image of Galactovision's holographic sports commentator, Rocco Wang, appeared on the monitor.

"Sorry for the interruption in our transmission from the Rawbone Rally, folks, but some of our equipment has short-circuited," Rocco Wang said.

"There's been a pile-up of vehicles at the start of the rally – a racer calling himself Zipzap has caused carnage down here. I've never seen anything like it!"

On the monitor, Cosmo saw destroyed vehicles behind Rocco, then the image wavered as the signal was lost again. "Zipzap's attacked the racers!" he exclaimed, blasting towards Opex's misshapen mass. Cosmo summoned his courage for the fight ahead and his spacesuit began to glow.

He was wearing the Quantum

Mutation Suit, G-Watch's most advanced combat system – a spacesuit that could transform him into alien beings to take on any opponent. It was activated by a power inside Cosmo, the power of the universe, that was present in all living things but uniquely strong in him.

"What do we know about this invader, Brain-E?" he asked.

The brainbot swivelled its stalk-eyes. "Well, according to G-Watch probes, Zipzap is an electric speed-freak, Master Cosmo, able to generate lightning bolts from his supercharged body."

Yikes! So he could electrocute us! Cosmo thought, alarmed. He gripped the steering column tightly and the Dragster 7000 shot through System Opex's outer atmosphere into swirling winds. Cosmo struggled to keep control as the ship bounced up and down in high turbulence.

"Opex's weather is violent and

changeable, Master Cosmo," Brain-E warned, sliding across the control desk as the spaceship juddered.

"The rally's start is southeast of here," Nuri said, checking the navigation console.

Cosmo adjusted course, flying the Dragster through a shower of hail stones; abruptly the hail ceased and blinding sunlight flooded the cockpit. Cosmo

squinted, but then the spacescreen darkened as black storm clouds engulfed the Dragster. Conditions were changing rapidly. Visibility was almost zero.

Cosmo glanced at the navigation console and saw the Moving Mountains of Antram, the starting point for the rally, indicated below. “We’re nearing the strike site. I’m taking us down,” he said.

"Look out for Zipzap."

As the Dragster descended through the clouds, Cosmo peered through the spacescreen and saw wreckage below: a huge crater in the ground and vehicles overturned, sparking with electricity. There was no sign of Zipzap, but as the spaceship touched down on the planet's surface Cosmo spotted Rocco Wang interviewing racers who'd crashed out of the rally. He turned off the Dragster's engines, opened the cockpit door and climbed out to talk to the holographic commentator. "Mr Wang, we're from G-Watch," he called. "What exactly happened here?"

Rocco Wang glanced at a small winged camera hovering beside him. "A G-Watch agent at the Rawbone! Things are even more serious than I thought, folks!" he announced. He turned to face Cosmo. "A crazy rider calling himself Zipzap entered the race, that's what happened!

He knocked out eight cars!"

"That rider's an alien invader sent by a galactic outlaw called Kaos," Cosmo explained, noticing more galactocams flying overhead, broadcasting his every word to the galaxy.

"You heard it here first, folks," Rocco Wang said, speaking to the galactocams. "The last-minute entrant is an alien invader. Which means one thing for this year's racers: DANGER!"

Cosmo looked across the trail of damaged vehicles to the Moving Mountains of Antram. The narrow gorges between them were moving continually, sending rocks tumbling down their sides. "Nuri, we've got to go after Zipzap before he causes any more harm," he called.

Nuri and Brain-E were checking out a dented DAX all-terrain buggy that had been toppled in the strike. Its ape-like Virilian driver and navigator were being treated by a rally ambulance crew.

"Nice car," Nuri said to the driver. "Can we borrow it?"

"Its ignition's blown," he replied gruffly. "It won't start."

"Allow me, Miss Nuri," Brain-E said, scuttling up onto the rally car's dashboard and inserting a probe arm into its controls. With a roar the DAX's engine started and the Virilian driver stared, open-mouthed with surprise.

"We'll bring it back in one piece," Nuri said to him. She winked at Cosmo. "You drive. I'll navigate."

Cosmo jumped into the driver's seat. With Nuri beside him and Brain-E on the dashboard, he gripped the rally car's steering bar and pressed his foot down hard on the accelerator. "We're coming for you, Zipzap!" he yelled as the DAX sped towards the mountains. "G-Watch is entering the race!"

CHAPTER TWO

THE DAX

"Go, Cosmo!" Nuri called from the navigator's seat.

The DAX powered past the wrecked rally cars and shot into a narrow gorge between two of the Moving Mountains of Antram. As the buggy's six wheels sped across the ground, Cosmo glanced up at towering walls of solid rock on each side. A rumbling sound echoed all around, and rocks clattered down from the moving mountains onto the bonnet.

"Uh-oh, the mountains are squeezing together; this gorge is closing!" Nuri cried.

"Like a giant car crusher!" Brain-E whimpered from the dashboard.

Cosmo pressed the accelerator hard to the floor, driving at top speed. He raced towards a vertical sliver of light about a kilometre ahead that marked the gorge's end. It was narrowing as the mountains closed in.

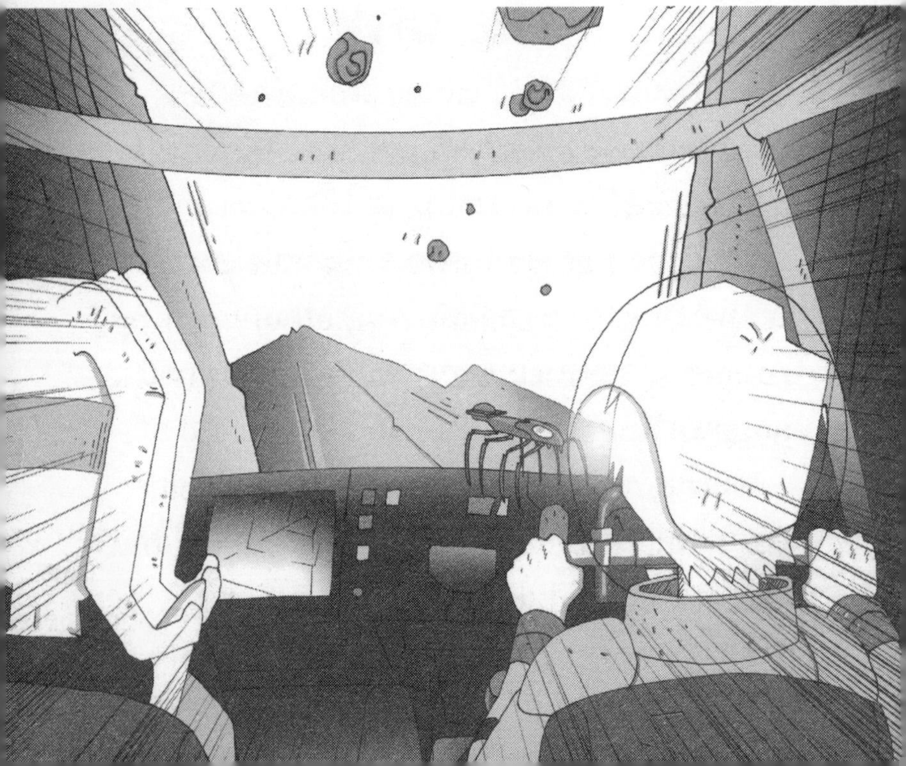

"Cosmo, can't this car go any faster?" Nuri asked, her voice rising in panic.

"I don't know," he replied, flipping open a panel on the dashboard, checking the DAX's controls. A touch-sensitive screen lit up displaying the car's all-terrain capabilities: GRIP MODE . . . GLIDER MODE . . . BOAT MODE . . . SKI MODE . . . WALK MODE . . . TURBO MODE . . . *Turbo mode!* "Here we go!"

He pressed the touchscreen and the buggy surged forward like a rocket, flames shooting from its rear as turbo thrusters ignited. "*Wooooo-hoooo!*" he cried, the acceleration pushing him back in his seat.

With the gorge narrowing either side of the Dax, there came a smell of burning rubber – the rock walls were touching the buggy's huge tyres.

"We'll never make it!" Brain-E cried, wrapping its legs around the steering bar and retracting its stalk-eyes in fear.

“Oh yes we will!” Cosmo called, directing the right wheels of the buggy over a fallen boulder using it as a ramp. The vehicle tipped up, its right-hand wheels now running along the wall of the gorge, its left-hand wheels still on the ground.

Driving the DAX on its side, Cosmo squeezed it through the narrowing gorge at high speed. He shot out into misty marshland, hearing a *BOOM!* from behind as the gorge slammed shut.

Cosmo pumped his foot on the brake, and the DAX skidded to a stop, bumping down onto all six wheels. "This is one *cool* car," he said, his heart thumping.

"And that was *cool* driving too, Cosmo," Nuri added.

Brain-E extended its stalk-eyes nervously, peering into the mist. "We made it through, but where are we now?" the little brainbot said.

Cosmo noticed the marshy ground ahead, churned up by the tyres of rally vehicles. "This looks like the Bog of Dral," he said, recognizing the place from previous years of watching the Rawbone Rally on Galactovision. "It's dotted with hidden sinking spots and if we drive into one there's no getting out." Cosmo flipped open the panel to the touchscreen and pressed WALK MODE. Clunks and whirrs came from the DAX's undercarriage and the vehicle rose, lifting Cosmo, Nuri and Brain-E aloft on six articulated hydraulic legs.

"What are you doing, Master Cosmo?" Brain-E asked.

"The DAX's walk mode should help us cross the marshland," Cosmo replied, pressing his foot to the accelerator. The vehicle's legs moved like an insect's, and it stalked slowly forward, each foot testing the marshy ground as it trod. When Cosmo felt a squelch he steered left or right to avoid the treacherous sinking spots.

Brain-E peered down over the dashboard, seeing the buggy's metal legs moving just like its own. "Oh, I like this, Master Cosmo. This is neat," it said.

As the DAX advanced with careful strides, Cosmo peered down and gulped, glimpsing the front end of a jet-kart protruding from the marsh. Galactocams hovered overhead, filming its drivers as they clambered out.

"It looks like some of the cars got stuck,"

Brain-E said, pointing to another: a trapped rocket-roller, its rider sitting on the roof waiting for rescue vehicles to arrive.

Cosmo noticed scorch marks on the roller's paintwork, then more on a stricken ten-wheeler, and a K-cruiser up ahead flickering with electricity like it had been struck by lightning. "These vehicles didn't all drive off course. Zipzap caused this!"

"He'll knock every rider out of the race if we don't catch him soon," Nuri added.

"Mountain ahead!" Brain-E cried, pointing with one of its metal legs into the mist.

In the distance, Cosmo could just make out the ground sloping upwards marking the end of the marshland. He steered the DAX past more wrecked vehicles then safely onto firm ground, where he tapped the touchscreen to revert to NORMAL MODE. "Navigation check, please, Nuri," he said as the buggy's legs retracted and it sank down to the ground.

Nuri tapped the navigation console, and an electronic map appeared on the screen, the DAX marked on it by a red dot. "We're now at the foot of the Svalbaz Ice Mountains," she said, tracing her finger to hundreds of dots moving among the mountain peaks. "The other racers are about fifty kilometres ahead."

Cosmo glanced at the dots, wondering where Zipzap was among them. He pressed his foot to the accelerator speeding up the steep mountainside.

The air turned cold as they got higher, and snowflakes began falling through the buggy's open top. Cosmo saw ice glinting on the ground ahead, then felt the DAX slide a little, its wheels skidding. He tapped the screen and switched to GRIP MODE, causing spikes to fan out from the wheel rims and dig into the icy ground. Cosmo maintained speed, driving over the ice onto a snow-packed trail. Higher and higher they climbed, a snowy blizzard now blowing around them. Then the trail levelled out a little, curving around the mountainside, and when Cosmo looked down he saw that only centimetres separated his side of the buggy from a steep snowy drop.

"We're going faster than the other racers," Nuri said, looking up from the console.

Cosmo sped round an icy bend, hearing a loud rumble from a peak above. "What was that?" he asked, glancing up.

Brain-E bleeped, its lights flashing anxiously. "Master Cosmo, I'm detecting tremors in the mountains around us."

"You mean they're moving too?"

"All environments on System Opex are unstable," the brainbot reminded him.

Cosmo squinted up through the blizzard, glimpsing a huge white mass tumbling from the mountain peak above. The rumbling grew louder. It was snow, tonnes of it, sliding down the side of the mountain towards them.

"Avalanche!" he cried.

CHAPTER
THREE

AVALANCHE!

The huge wave of snow thundered down, sweeping the DAX off the mountain track.

Nuri grabbed hold of Brain-E to stop the little brainbot falling out as the buggy was shunted down the drop, enveloped by careering snow.

"We'll be buried alive!" Brain-E cried.

Cosmo, shuddering in his seat, reached for the controls and pressed SKI MODE on the touchscreen. Instantly the DAX's

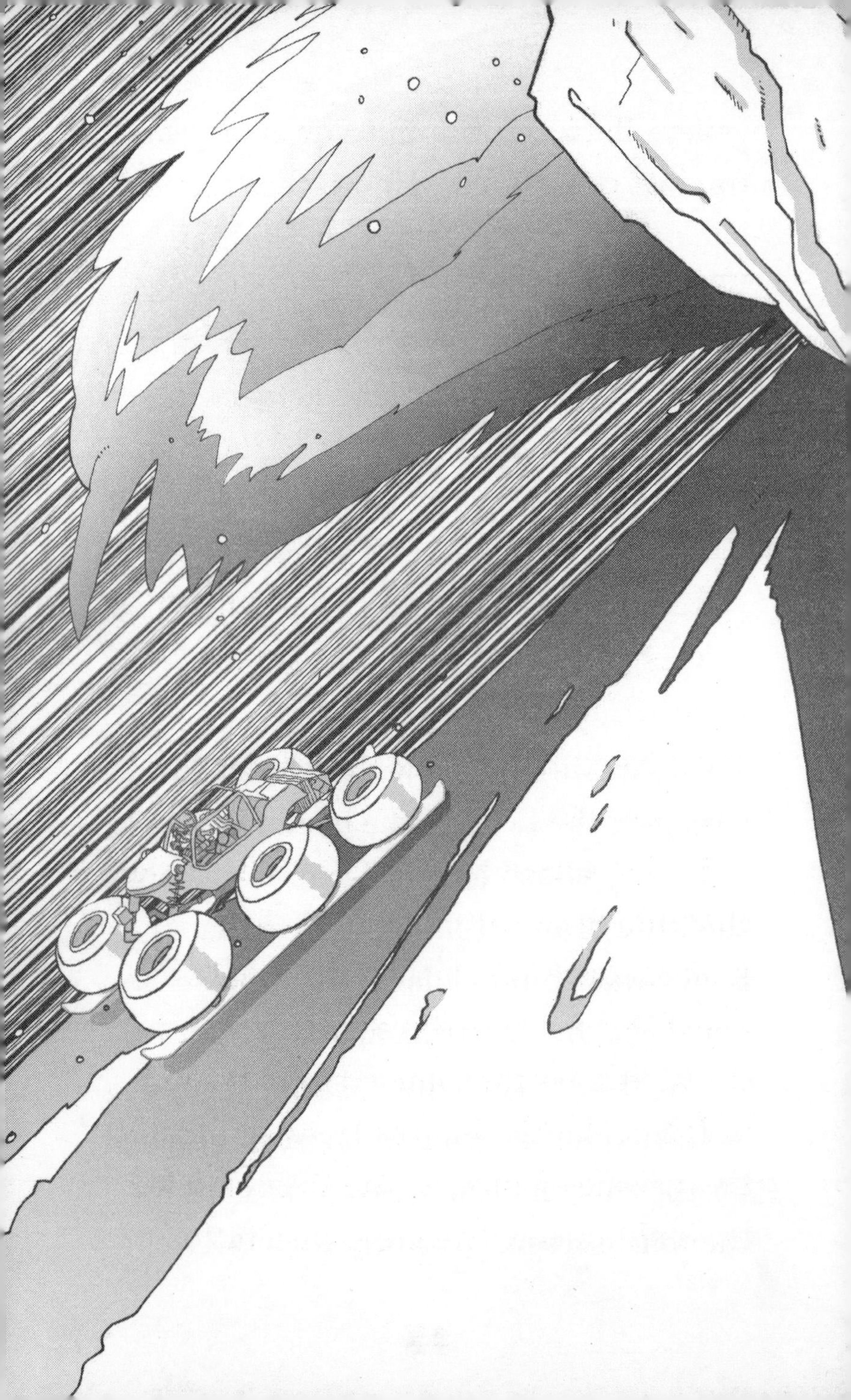

wheels flattened out and skis emerged from its chassis. He gripped the steering bar, driving the buggy like a Ski-Doo. With a rev of the DAX's engines, the skis surged over the powdery snow, speeding downwards as if on a slide. Faster and faster they went, fleeing the avalanche down the steep mountain drop.

"Yeeeeeee-haaaaaa!" Nuri cried.

Towards the mountain's base the slope levelled out. The DAX's skis slid towards a line of green trees.

"Drive into those trees for protection," Nuri advised.

Cosmo accelerated as fast as he could, outrunning the avalanche. The icy ground turned to slush then to leaves as the DAX sped between the trees. Loud cracks and booms sounded from behind as the avalanche hit, the trees acting like a barricade against it. The DAX skidded to a halt among lush green vegetation.

Cosmo felt warm air around him now, and heard chirruping insects and tropical birdsong. Sweat trickled down his neck. "The climate on System Opex certainly is changeable," he said, glancing around in astonishment, spotting brightly coloured alien flowers, giant butterflies, and long-beaked birds.

Nuri checked the map on the navigation console to see where they were. "We've been knocked off course into the Kervu Jungle," she said. "Head west and we can pick up the rally route as it comes down off the Ice Mountains."

"Sure thing," Cosmo replied, retracting the DAX's skis and re-engaging its wheels.

THUD! What looked like a huge coconut dropped to the ground close by. Cosmo glanced up into the jungle trees. Their branches were swaying as blue alien monkeys leaped among them, knocking the large nuts off.

THUD! One bounced off the DAX's bonnet.

"We should get a move on, Master Cosmo," Brain-E suggested, peering nervously at the deep dent it had made.

Cosmo pressed his foot to the accelerator and sped away between the trees, leaving the monkeys behind. He swerved around a massive dollop of steaming dung. "That's huge! What animal did that, Brain-E?" he asked.

Brain-E shone its scanner light over the buggy's side. "A saurex," it replied.

"What's a saurex?"

But before the brainbot had time to answer, a loud roar echoed from behind and there came a sound of heavy pounding footsteps. Cosmo glanced back and saw a huge alien dinosaur crashing through the trees towards them, its jaws wide open.

Brain-E flashed its lights in panic.

"Master Cosmo, *that's* a saurex!"

The beast lunged for the DAX, ripping off the rear fender, crunching it in its jaws.

"Friendly thing, isn't it?" Cosmo said, speeding away through the jungle. But the saurex continued thundering after them, its mighty jaws snapping.

"Try turbo mode!" Brain-E cried.

"Too risky with these trees around," Cosmo replied.

Suddenly Cosmo saw the bend of a wide river ahead and veered along its bank. The saurex was still right on their tail. Cosmo realized that the river flowed west, and it gave him an idea. He turned the steering bar, sending the DAX flying off the riverbank and splashing into the water. While the saurex roared at them from the bank, the buggy drifted away safely in the current.

"Good escape, Cosmo – but now what?" Nuri asked.

Cosmo pressed the touchscreen, activating BOAT MODE, and the DAX's wheels retracted, propellers appearing in their place as it turned into a speedboat. "The river flows west, Nuri. It should lead us back towards the race." He accelerated and the DAX's propellers turned faster, powering them through the water.

Nuri checked the navigation console, seeing a few dozen dots exiting the Ice

Mountains. "Smart move, Cosmo. The rally racers appear to be heading for the Torgen Desert," she said. "It looks like there have been lots of casualties. Fewer than fifty cars are left in the race now."

"Zipzap's running amok!" Cosmo exclaimed. He gripped the steering bar, speeding down the river as fast as he could.

The jungle air grew hotter and drier, and soon the trees started to thin out. Sand lined the riverbank, and jungle shrubs gave way to spiky cacti. The river became shallower, its water evaporating into steam in the heat.

"The river's drying up," Nuri said.

Soon it was just a trickle, the water running off into cracks in the dry ground.

The DAX's hull scraped to a standstill and Cosmo re-engaged the wheels, driving onto the dry sand of the Torgen Desert. He squinted in the bright sunshine. A couple of kilometres away, he could just make out a line of rally cars. He pressed his foot to the floor and sped after them. "Hold tight!" he said. "We're back in the race!"

CHAPTER
FOUR

THE RACE IS ON!

Adrenaline pumping, Cosmo blasted across the desert at turbo speed. He sped after the rally racers looking for Zipzap. He overtook a pointed V9 land-rocket, then a marsh-racer powered by a huge rear fan. He shot between a group of rugged dirt-wheelers and swerved past an armoured roadster on racing caterpillar tracks. Galactocams buzzed overhead, broadcasting the race to viewers all over the galaxy.

“This is more like it!” Nuri said as they overtook a three-wheeled biker, then a DVC off-roader, its driver gripping the wheel with red tentacles.

The DAX was covering ground fast now, but the only signs of Zipzap were car wrecks flickering with electricity. Cosmo passed an overturned slick-wagon, the driver and navigator marooned inside it, then swerved round a scorched land-schooner and a Titan sixteen-wheeler, its tyres melted and buckled.

“Zipzap’s causing carnage,” Cosmo said.

“And who knows how many billions of people are watching on Galactovision,” Nuri added, pointing to the galactocams zipping overhead in the heat, filming everything.

Cosmo gripped the steering bar tightly as a hot wind buffeted the DAX, bringing with it swirling sand.

Brain-E bleeped in alarm. “Oh goodness, Master Cosmo! It’s a sandstorm!”

Up ahead, a frigate-truck was picked up by the wind and hurled aside as the storm ripped towards them. Galactocams went spinning in the swirling air, and Cosmo ducked as one whizzed past his head and fell into the back of the DAX.

Brain-E scuttled to check on it. “Oh dear, its lens is smashed,” it said. “It’s broken.”

The brainbot scuttled back and clamped itself to Nuri's harness for protection.

"I'm losing control in these winds," Cosmo said, fighting with the steering bar.

"Just keep trying, Cosmo," Nuri said, protecting her face with her hands and peering between her fingers at the navigation console. "Hold a westerly course until we've crossed the desert."

With the sandstorm now engulfing the Dax, Cosmo held the steering bar firm, driving blind in the swirling winds. He kept his foot to the pedal, with only one thought on his mind: *Zipzap's still in the race, and it's up to me to stop him.*

CHAPTER
FIVE

TIME FOR CRITTER CRISPS

Meanwhile, far beyond the galaxy in the Wrecking Zone, the five-headed outlaw Kaos was in the cockpit of the battleship *Oblivion* reclining in a whalax-skull chair, sipping a blood-red drink and stuffing his faces with fried critter crisps.

"Turn on Galactovision, Wugrat," Kaos's first head said to a purple rat sitting with him. "Let's enjoy the race."

The rat squeaked in reply, "Eeeek,"

and scratched at the buttons of a remote control. On a large monitor, video footage appeared of rally cars racing across a sandy desert, speeding into a swirling

sandstorm. An image of Rocco Wang appeared alongside them.

"It's that idiotic Rawbone commentator! Turn it up," Kaos's third head said. "Let's hear what he has to say."

Wugrat scratched at the remote control, turning up the volume.

"Time for a round-up, rally fans," Rocco Wang said. "Rawbone racers are crashing out faster than we can count – they're being attacked by an invader called Zipzap . . ."

"Ha! Ha!" Kaos's fourth head laughed.

"Shocking images picked up by our galactocams show the rebel racer's trail of destruction. What a fiend he is!" The screen cut to images of wrecked rally cars, then to a large mono-wheeled alien sparking like lightning. "Also in the race is G-Watch's Agent Supreme, Cosmo Santos, who says that this invader has been sent on the orders of an outlaw named Kaos."

"He said our name on Galactovision – we're famous!" Kaos's first head yelped excitedly.

"Yes, you heard it here first, folks: G-Watch versus Kaos. This isn't just a rally any more. This is war!"

"This is perfect," Kaos's fourth head murmured. "Just as I planned. Now fear will spread far and wide."

"It's rather a fun plan too," Kaos's second head added.

"It's not only fun, it's brilliant!" the fourth head replied. "By the time the Rawbone Rally is finished, the whole galaxy will know of our power. Zipzap will be victorious and that Earthling boy will be destroyed on Galactovision for everyone to see!" Kaos stuffed his mouths with critter crisps and grinned wickedly as he settled back to watch the race.

* * *

Back on Opex, Cosmo headed through the desert sandstorm, with Nuri beside him desperately trying to check the route. The storm gusted, sometimes allowing Cosmo a glimpse ahead but mostly obscuring his view, and the noise in his helmet was deafening as sand clattered against it. Once or twice he had to swerve suddenly to avoid a sparking wreck stuck in the swirling sand, and all the time he knew that Zipzap must be close.

Cosmo felt the storm subsiding slightly, the DAX being buffeted less, and he sped up, his foot pressed hard on the accelerator. The buggy bumped and bounced as the terrain beneath it altered. He glanced down and, with the storm lessening, glimpsed clumps of long grass growing up through the sand.

"Grasslands!" Nuri said. "We're approaching the Zilfa Savannah."

Cosmo breathed a sigh of relief as the

sandstorm cleared and he saw Opex's two suns shining from the purple sky onto lush green grasslands, vehicles speeding across them. On either side of the DAX, dented and battered rally cars jostled for position.

"Did we make it safely out of the storm?" Brain-E asked, extending its stalk-eyes.

"Not only that, but we must be closing in on Zipzap," Cosmo replied, swerving past an overturned Colossus roadster sparking with electricity, its wheels still spinning as if it had only just crashed.

Cosmo opened his visor and clean air rushed in as he bumped over ruts ripped into the ground by the speeding wheels of the rally cars. Ahead, a herd of big orange hairy beasts was grazing. They looked a little like a cross between buffalo and woolly mammoths.

The brainbot peered out at them.

“They’re kuffalox,” it said. “Herbivores – nothing to be afraid of.”

Cosmo weaved through the herd of beasts, glancing at the navigation console and seeing six moving dots ahead of the Dax. *Just six racers left in the rally*, he realized. *And Zipzap has to be among them*. But as he looked past the kuffalox, trying to spot the invader on the savannah,

his view was obscured by ash and smoke drifting from belching volcanoes.

Nuri reached for the DAX's roll-bar, pulling herself up. She stood on her seat, peering into the distance.

"What are you doing?" Cosmo asked her.

Nuri's sensitive Etrusian ears twitched. "I can hear something ahead," she said.

"What?" Cosmo called, straining to

hear anything above the kuffalox grunts and the noise from the DAX's engine.

"Wings!" Nuri told him.

Out of the volcanic ash clouds, a flock of enormous yellow creatures appeared, each as large as a plane. They had long sharp beaks and leathery wings like flying reptiles of prey, and they circled high above, eyeing the kuffalox.

"Uh-oh," Brain-E said, extending its stalk eyes upwards. "Lavadactyls, System Opex's largest avian predators."

Nuri nervously sat down again.

All at once the lavadactyls began to attack. One swooped down and clasped a grazing kuffalox in its talons, then carried the beast high into the grey sky.

"They're feeding!" Brain-E said.

"Watch out, Cosmo!" Nuri cried as a lavadactyl flew down and grabbed the DAX's roll-bar.

"Now it thinks *we're* lunch!" Cosmo

said, swerving left and right, trying to shake the creature off. But the lavadactyl beat its huge yellow wings and lifted the DAX off the ground. Up and up they soared, into the smoky sky.

CHAPTER
SIX

THE RED MOUNTAINS

Cosmo looked up at the huge talons gripping the DAX's roll-bar. The creature was enormous. Its wings lifted it through the ash-filled air, soaring high above the savannah towards the smoking volcanoes.

"Lavadactyls are flameproof and live *in* the volcanoes," Brain-E said. "But if it takes *us* there we'll be toasted."

Cosmo could feel the heat of the volcanoes even from a distance. He saw red-hot lava spewing into the air. "Whoa, I don't like this!" he said.

"We've got to get out of the DAX now!" Nuri cried.

Cosmo looked down, wondering whether to jump. He could make out rally vehicles far below, like toys. *It's too high. We'll be splatted*, he thought. The vehicles were skirting the edge of the volcanoes,

dodging lava bombs and heading for a row of tooth-like mountains. They disappeared from sight as the lavadactyl carried the DAX into an ash cloud. Everything went pitch dark.

"Cosmo, I've got an idea," Nuri yelled beside him through the black smoke.

He heard a buzzing sound, then saw a bright red laser light above his head. Nuri was using a laser cutter from her utility belt to slice through the DAX's metal roll-bar. Carefully avoiding the sharp talons of the lavadactyl, she cut through one side of the bar, and the buggy tipped. Then she started on the other side.

"But, Nuri, we'll fall," Cosmo said, alarmed. No sooner had he spoken than she cut through the other side of the roll-bar. A chunk of it snapped off and the buggy suddenly dropped out of the grip of the lavadactyl.

"Aaaaaaarghhh!" Cosmo's body jerked upwards in his driving harness, ash and smoke swirling around him as the DAX plummeted. He saw a light appear on the touchscreen and Nuri's hand pressing a button: GLIDE MODE. Wings extended from the sides of the buggy, and Cosmo felt them catching the air, slowing their descent. The DAX was gliding!

"Nice work, Nuri," he said. But suddenly the ash cloud thinned and he glimpsed a mountainside ahead. "Hold tight!" he called, turning the steering bar sharply, trying to steer the DAX away; but its left wing clipped a rocky outcrop and sheered off. "Brace yourselves!"

Down they fell, tumbling against the mountainside, and with a sickening *CRUNCH!* came to a standstill on a rocky ledge, where the DAX's engine cut out. "Sorry about that, folks," Cosmo said, pressing the touchscreen to revert to

NORMAL MODE. But the buggy's controls weren't responding. The screen was blank.

Nuri flicked a row of switches and Brain-E inserted a probe arm into the dashboard, but still nothing happened.

"The impact must have damaged the DAX's circuits," the brainbot explained. "None of its systems are working."

"Can it be fixed?" Cosmo asked.

"It will take time," Brain-E replied.

Cosmo clambered out and examined the vehicle. One wing had snapped off and the front fender was crumpled. He glanced up at the high mountains all around. "Where are we? We must be way off track."

"There's no way of finding out," Nuri said. "The navigation console is down."

"I have an idea," Brain-E said. The brainbot scuttled over to the broken galactocam that had been blown into the buggy by the desert storm and began unscrewing its top.

"What are you doing?" Cosmo asked.

"This galactocam contains a transmitter that sends images to Galactovision," Brain-E replied. "If I can reverse it, we may be able to pick up Galactovision's signal to locate the racers."

Cosmo glanced at Nuri, who shrugged her shoulders as if baffled.

Brain-E selected a component from inside the broken galactocam and inserted it upside-down into its own holographic imager. The brainbot bleeped

then projected a video image – live from Galactovision – of rally cars speeding down a mountain. Rocco Wang was hovering above the action, speaking to camera: “And as the lead racers head over the Red Mountains, the crazy mono-rider, Zipzap, is closing in! Surely they’ll be zapped too? Still no sign of the DAX. It looks as if G-Watch are out of this race!”

The image became fuzzy, then was gone. “Signal lost,” Brain-E said.

"Very smart, Brain-E, but we still don't know where *we* are," Nuri remarked.

"There must be something we can do," Cosmo said desperately. Just then he noticed that the mountain they were standing on was made of red rock. "Hey, Rocco Wang said the leaders were heading over the *Red* Mountains. Perhaps we're not so far off the pace after all." With growing excitement, he climbed up the steep mountainside to look over a nearby ridge. Sure enough, more red mountains stretched out before him like a row of teeth, a track zigzagging among them.

And about three kilometres away, Cosmo could make out rally cars! He unclipped a hawkeye monocular from his utility belt and peered through it. Axel Crock was in the lead, then came Ji-Phon, then Zimla Cordosa. Closing on them, in a cloud of dust, was a massive sparking metal alien riding a mono-wheel. *Zipzap!*

Cosmo saw the invader shoot a bolt of lightning at Zimla Cordosa's rally car, and it exploded in a bright flash of blue light, tumbling out of the race.

"Nuri, you and Brain-E try to repair the DAX. I'm going after Zipzap on foot!"

"On foot? But you'll never catch up."

"Yes I will, Nuri. It's time for me to use the Quantum Mutation Suit!"

CHAPTER
SEVEN

A SUPERFAST WILDCAT!

Cosmo spoke the command into his helmet's sensor: "SCAN." Digital images of aliens flashed on his visor as the Quantum Mutation Suit searched through its databank: a razor-tusked earthmover . . . a spurred svatava . . . a stinking dzik . . . *Which alien can catch a rebel racer?* he wondered. He assessed their heights, weights and features, then focused on an image of a six-legged alien wildcat:

A superfast wildcat! Perfect! Cosmo thought. "MUTATE!"

Suddenly he felt his body tingle as the Quantum Mutation Suit meshed with his flesh, his molecules changing into those of Panthrax. His muscles grew, two extra limbs pushing from his sides, and his arms thickened into legs. He had six running legs, and his toenails sharpened into claws. Thick black hair sprouted over his skin, and long curved teeth split through his gums. He sprang into action, racing after Zipzap.

As Panthrax, Cosmo was fast and agile across the rocky terrain, sprinting over the mountains with ease. He didn't follow the zigzagging trail of the rally riders, but raced straight up and down near-vertical slopes, gripping with his claws and leaping with outstretched limbs. He quickly gained on the vehicles; and all the while galactocams whizzed overhead broadcasting his pursuit live.

Ahead, Zipzap fired a volley of lightning bolts at Ji-Phon's land-sloop. Ji-Phon ejected just as his vehicle exploded in a flash of light. Cosmo swerved to avoid one of the sloop's wheels as it came bouncing down. He bounded faster on his six wildcat legs, gaining on the rebel racer. He could taste the alien's exhaust fumes in his mouth, and the dust from the invader's spinning mono-wheel stung his eyes. "Zipzap, in the name of G-Watch, stop!" he ordered.

Zipzap glanced round, surprised to see his challenger so close. "I've been warned of

your powers, freak boy. You'll not stop me!"

The alien shot a lightning bolt at Cosmo, but Cosmo dodged and – *BAM!* – it scorched the ground beside him. Zipzap fired and missed again, blasting a boulder to dust. Cosmo put on a burst of speed and leaped for the invader's tyre, slicing its thick rubber with his wildcat claws.

Zipzap swerved as the shredded rubber tyre spun off his monowheel, but he kept racing, screeching along on the metal rims. The mighty alien turned, his body sparking, electricity fizzing from his metal hands. "G-Watch is weak! Kaos is strong!" he bellowed into a galactocam that flew overhead, filming the battle.

Cosmo launched himself at the alien again, his wildcat claws extended, but Zipzap struck him with a high-voltage blast and the shock sent Cosmo tumbling.

He tried to get to his feet but was unable to move, his wildcat muscles twitching from the electric shock, his nerves sparking and jangling, and his fur smoking. Cosmo watched helplessly as the invader disappeared over a peak in pursuit of the leader, Axel Crock. He tried to move his limbs but was now powerless.

"RESET," he managed to say. The Quantum Mutation Suit activated, and Panthrax's molecular pattern broke up, healing the effects of the electric shock, as Cosmo changed back into his boy self.

He got to his feet and ran after Zipzap, scrambling up the peak. He looked down a long winding slope that led from the Red Mountains to an open plain scorched dry by Opex's twin suns. In the distance, at the plain's end, stood two enormous stone pillars – the Pillars of Rawbone – that marked the race's finish line. Zipzap was zigzagging down the slope at speed, now just behind the leader, Axel Crock. With a *BOOM!* the invader shot a bolt of lightning at Axel's chain-wheeler, and its undercarriage burst into flames. The champion rally driver leaped out of the

vehicle as its fuel tanks exploded. Cosmo gasped. Zipzap was now in first place!

"SCAN," Cosmo said, panic rising within him. Images of alien creatures flashed in front of his eyes: an exploding anona . . . an electric zhalo . . . a scissor-tongued kuras . . . *What can stop Zipzap once and for all?* he wondered. He spotted a craggy alien with a rock-hard body.

ALIEN: BOULDER
SPECIES: THUD
ORIGIN: ASTEROID E467
HEIGHT: 4 METRES
WEIGHT: 2 TONNES
FEATURE: ROCKHARD BODY

Boulder will pulverize Zipzap, Cosmo thought. "MUTATE!"

CHAPTER EIGHT

BOULDER

Cosmo felt his body tingle as the Quantum Mutation Suit fused with his flesh. His molecular structure re-formed; he grew bigger, his limbs and back becoming rough like rock, his muscles as hard as stone. He was Boulder the thud, and he felt strong.

He glanced down the steep slope, seeing Zipzap speeding towards the open plain. He made a quick calculation, plotting his trajectory, then flexed his stony thuddian muscles and called to a galactocam that was filming above: "Boulder is going to squish Zipzap!"

Cosmo leaped over the edge and curled his body into a ball. He bounced on the rocky mountainside . . . once . . . twice . . . and began rolling down the steep slope, his huge boulder-like body smashing rocks as he spun head over heels. He was picking up speed all the time, hurtling downwards, faster and faster, in a dizzying blur.

He tumbled onto the open plain, with just Zipzap ahead of him – he was on a collision course for the invader!

Cosmo braced himself as he smashed straight into the invader. The force of the mighty collision sent both of them crashing and tumbling across the dusty plain.

Cosmo rolled away over the ground and slowly came to a stop. He uncurled his rocky thuddian body and lay motionless for a moment, cracked and weakened by the impact. The sky and the clouds appeared to spin above him, galactocams swirling in a blur. "RESET," he gasped, transforming back into a boy.

Cosmo glanced across the dry plain to see what was left of Zipzap. The invader lay on his front, battered and dented, his wheel detached, electrical energy flickering from his broken body. The alien stretched out his arm and began dragging himself across the ground.

He's reaching for his wheel, Cosmo realized . . . Cosmo tried to get to his feet to stop the alien, but staggered, dizzy from the massive collision. He heard a buggy approaching, then phaser fire streaked in . . . It was Nuri in the DAX! She had got it working again and was hurtling down the mountain track, firing her phaser gun at the invader. But the blasts ricocheted off Zipzap's body.

"Ha! G-Watch weapons won't defeat me!" Zipzap roared. He grabbed hold of his detached wheel and pushed it back onto its bent axle, his metallicon flesh meshing with it once again. "I am unstoppable!" He revved his engine and, in a cloud of dust, sped off towards the Pillars of Rawbone.

How am I ever going to beat that metallicon? Cosmo thought desperately, still in a daze.

Nuri skidded to a halt beside him, and the DAX's passenger door flew open. "Get in, Cosmo!" She reached over and pulled him into the buggy then hit the TURBO MODE button and they sped off after the alien.

"Are you OK, Master Cosmo?" Brain-E asked. "You look a bit pale."

"Zipzap's a tough enemy," Cosmo replied.

"Well, he hasn't won yet," Nuri said.

They were gaining on the invader. "I'll give you cover, Cosmo. The rest is down to you!"

Steering with one hand and holding her phaser gun in the other, Nuri opened fire on the alien. Phaser blasts pummelled Zipzap's metal body. He raised his supercharged arm, ready to retaliate with a lightning bolt, but Nuri hit him again, causing him to miss.

Galactocams flew overhead, transmitting images of everything that was happening. The Pillars of Rawbone, the rally's finish, were now only a kilometre away.

All eyes are watching us, Cosmo thought. *I can't let this metalhead win*. "SCAN," he said into the sensor of the Quantum Mutation Suit. On the visor of his helmet, images of aliens appeared once more. Cosmo spotted a weird-looking alien with mirror-like skin.

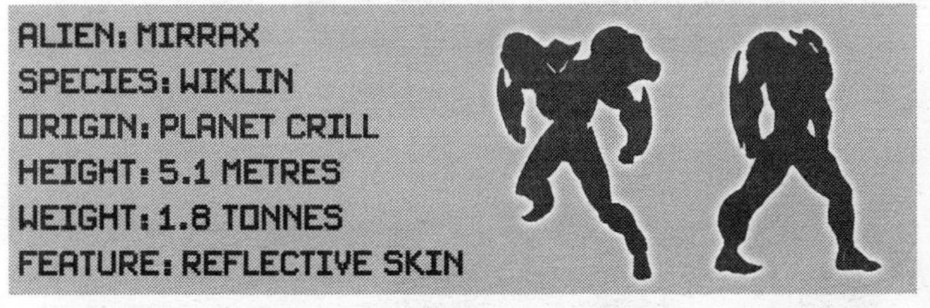

Reflective skin! Perhaps Mirrax could give Zipzap a blast of his own, Cosmo thought.

"Hold your fire, Nuri," he said, climbing onto the bonnet of the DAX. He summoned his strength one last time. "MUTATE!"

CHAPTER
NINE

THE PILLARS OF RAWBONE

Speeding along on the bonnet of the DAX, Cosmo felt the molecules in his body mutating. His skin crusted over becoming golden glass, his arms and legs flattening and shining like mirrors. His entire body was now a reflective shield; the bright sunlight glinted off him.

As Nuri brought the buggy alongside the invader, Cosmo called to Zipzap: "Hey, Sparky, think you can beat G-Watch?"

"There can be only one winner here, and that's ME!" Zipzap replied. He fired a lightning bolt directly at Cosmo, but Mirrax blocked it with his reflective arm. His mirror skin sent the lightning bolt bouncing straight off.

"Missed!" Cosmo called.

Zipzap shot another bolt of lightning, and Cosmo raised his other arm, deflecting that too.

"Is that the best you can do?" he shouted, then glanced ahead. They were only a hundred metres from the finish line. Dozens of galactocams were still flying overhead, videoing the action. "Come on, give it your best shot, Zit-splat!"

Enraged, Zipzap raised both hands and fired massive twin bolts of lightning.

Cosmo stuck out his chest and felt the full force of the double strike thud against him. The energy was immense and it almost toppled him, sending shockwaves through his body, but he held firm as his reflective skin flashed, shooting the double strike straight back at Zipzap.

It hit the invader in a burst of bright

blue light, and he let out an earsplitting roar: "AAAAAAARGH!" His engine exploded and he skidded along the ground on his side.

Cosmo leaped off the bonnet of the DAX as it came to a stop. His vision was a little blurred and he felt a smarting pain where his mirrored chest had cracked, but the invader was now weakened too.

Nuri came running from the buggy. "Cosmo, are you OK?" she asked.

Cosmo spoke the command, "RESET," and his mirror-like body tingled, his cracked skin healing, and his vision clearing as he turned back into an Earthling boy. He looked to see what had happened to Zipzap. A line of sparking scorch marks blackened the ground. The alien was dragging himself towards the finish line, his wheel buckled, his metalwork blackened and singed, his whole body fizzing.

Cosmo staggered over to the invader. "You're finished, Zipzap," he said.

"I'm still going to win this race," the

alien hissed. "The whole galaxy will see me beat G-Watch."

"You don't play fair," Cosmo said. He thought of all the drivers whose rally cars Zipzap had ruined, and the billions of viewers watching fearfully around the galaxy. He summoned the power inside him and his Quantum Mutation Suit began to glow. His gloved hand tingled, his power extending from it, forming a sword.

"Here – try handling the Power of the Universe," Cosmo said. He raised the power sword and plunged it into the invader.

Zipzap howled: "NOOOO!"

Cosmo felt his whole body shake, his power locked in battle with Zipzap's high-voltage electricity. The invader

glowed brighter and brighter. Then he began to fizz and smoke as his circuits overheated. With a loud *BANG!* Zipzap exploded in a flash of light, the force hurling Cosmo through the air.

Cosmo hit the ground and lay on his back, exhausted. He looked up at the sky and smiled. He had defeated Zipzap!

“Well done, Cosmo,” Nuri said, helping him up. “Mirrax was a genius mutation.”

Cosmo heard the whirr of galactocams above him, then the air shimmered and Rocco Wang fizzed into life. “And here we are at the finish line of the 207th Rawbone Rally,” the Galactovision commentator said. “A race that will always be remembered as the toughest Rawbone in history. Well, how does it feel to be the winner?” he asked Cosmo. “Would you care to say a few words to the galaxy about your victory?”

Victory? Cosmo looked around and saw that the explosion had knocked him across the finish line. He really *had* won the race! He stared into the galactocams. “It feels . . . kinda cool,” he said. And he thought of all the people around the galaxy who’d be tuning in. “Hi, Mum, if you’re watching. Don’t worry, I’m having a blast!”

* * *

Meanwhile, far beyond the galaxy, in the cockpit of the battleship *Oblivion*, Kaos sat staring at the monitor. Images were coming in of Rocco Wang talking to Cosmo on Galactovision.

"I feel sick," Kaos's first head spat.

"Turn it off!" his second head said.

"Zipzap lost!" moaned his third.

"Wugrat, TURN IT OFF!" the fourth head shrieked angrily.

The purple rat scurried to the remote control and scratched at the ON/OFF button. The monitor went blank.

Kaos slammed his fist down on the arm of the whalax-skull chair, smashing it to pieces. "That supercharged nitwit Zipzap has failed!" his fourth head said.

Kaos's fifth head snarled, "So now it's *my* turn." The fifth head looked at the other four. "Seeing how each of you dunderheads has failed with your plans, *I'm* going to send in Tanka to do the job!"

Kaos picked up a small circuit board then strode through the battleship to the cargo hold, where a mutant metallicon alien was waiting. It had a huge cannon blaster for an arm.

"Tanka, you're needed," Kaos's fifth head growled. He approached the metallicon with the circuit board, then pulled open a metal panel in the alien's chest, exposing throbbing metallic flesh.

"On this circuit board is encoded a plan so ruthless and brilliant that G1, the Chief of G-Watch himself, will be personally begging me for mercy," the fifth head said. Kaos thrust the circuit board elbow-deep inside Tanka, and in a sparking flash, the metallicon absorbed the wires and microchips. Kaos replaced the metal panel and the invader's metallic flesh bubbled up, soldering it shut. "You'd better not fail me," his fifth head warned the alien.

Tanka stared back. "Failure is not in

my programming, Master," he replied.

Kaos's fifth head grinned. "Excellent."

Wugrat scurried in with a crystal navicom transporter disc in its mouth. Kaos reached down and snatched it from the rat, then twisted its outer edge. He attached the navicom to Tanka, and it began to flash. The alien pointed his cannon arm upwards as the roof of the cargo hold opened, then, with a *whoosh*, he shot out of the battleship and vanished into space.

CHAPTER
TEN

G1'S NEWS

A Rawbone Rally rescue saucer picked up Cosmo, Nuri and Brain-E and airlifted them back to the Dragster. Sitting in the saucer with them were Rocco Wang and the stranded drivers from the lead pack.

"What a race!" Zimla Cordosa said, lifting her racing visor, revealing three green eyes.

"You're the best, Cosmo," Axel Crock said, patting him on the back with his paw.

"If you're ever on Planet Zoblon, drop by and we can go sloop-racing together," said Ji-Phon, his blue hair still sticking up on end from Zipzap's lightning strike.

Cosmo felt proud. He'd beaten Zipzap *and* won the Rawbone Rally! He hoped

his friends from school on Earth had been watching on Galactovision.

When they got back to the Moving Mountains of Antram where the rally had begun, Opex's twin suns were starting to set. The Dragster was parked there, and as the saucer landed beside it Cosmo said goodbye to the drivers. He climbed out of the rescue vehicle and boarded the G-Watch spaceship.

"Home sweet home," Nuri said, climbing aboard too and slumping into the co-pilot's seat.

"It feels good to be back," Cosmo remarked, running his hand across the Dragster's control desk. He switched on the communicator and put a call in to G-Watch headquarters.

The face of G1 appeared on the console, his silver eyes twinkling. A cheer rose from behind him as other G-Watch agents applauded to congratulate Cosmo.

"We watched the whole thing via Galactovision on the big screen, here, Cosmo," G1 said. "Everyone is very proud of what you've achieved."

Cosmo glanced at Brain-E and Nuri. "It was a team effort," he said.

G1 tried to smile but his brow furrowed and he hesitated to speak.

"Is something wrong, G1?" Cosmo asked.

"I'm afraid I have bad news: Kaos has dispatched his last invader, a metallicon called Tanka. Our scanners have detected him heading towards Planet Kefu in the Alpha Quadrant."

Nuri gasped. "But, G1, Planet Kefu is home to the Galactic Life Sanctuary."

"Sorry? What's that?" Cosmo asked, confused.

Brain-E bleeped. "A place of extreme scientific importance, Master Cosmo," it explained, "a wildlife reserve for rare and endangered galactic creatures."

"Leave this to us, G1," Cosmo said. "We'll go after this invader and destroy him."

"I know you will do your best, Agent Cosmo," G1 replied. "And may the Power of the Universe be stronger in you than it has ever been."

"You bet, G1. Over and out!"

Cosmo engaged the ship's thrusters and the Dragster blasted into the air, shooting up through the evening sky towards the stars. "Tanka, here we come!"

Join Cosmo on his next **ALIEN INVADERS** mission. He must face – and defeat

TANKA

THE BALLISTIC BLASTER

INVADER ALERT!

In the cargo hold of an interstellar livestock transporter, Ranger Cron kept watch over a waking meglaphant: a mighty mammoth-like beast being transported from the thawing ice-planet Slok to the Galactic Life Sanctuary on Planet Kefu. The beast seemed agitated after its journey, and swung its long trunk against the wall of the hold.

"There, there. You're nearly at your new home," Ranger Cron said, stroking the beast's white fur with his scaly Kefuan hand.

He reached to one of its tusks to steady himself as the ship landed with a jolt. The engines quietened and hydraulic bolts unlocked at the back of the hold, a large exit ramp opening downwards. Bright daylight flooded in and Ranger Cron led the meglaphant out onto the straw-covered landing area of a warm forested planet. The beast trumpeted contentedly.

"Happy to have arrived, eh?" Ranger Cron said to it. "You'll like it here, I promise. This is just the start of things."

More transporter ships were landing

too, ramps lowering from them and other alien creatures being led out by Life Sanctuary rangers: emerald-and-black zebraves from the shrinking Planet Bol; giant meteor slugs from storma-space; a herd of walrakk from the polluted seas of Organa, and even hairy ape-flowers and giant walking goak trees. All were being led across the landing area to large stone pyramids among the trees.

Ranger Cron guided the meglaphant towards a vast footbath of disinfectant where a ranger was checking the creatures in. "An adult male meglaphant for sanctuary dimension C19," Ranger Cron called.

More rangers were hosing the creatures down, ensuring no infectious diseases would be brought into the wildlife sanctuary from across the galaxy.

But just as Ranger Cron reached the disinfection area, the meglaphant stopped walking. "Come on, it's only a footbath," Ranger Cron said, gently tugging the beast's fur to encourage it on.

The other creatures began behaving oddly too: birds screeched, zebraves bolted and walrakk bellowed, all clearly agitated.

Amidst their noise the meglaphant raised its trunk to the sky, trumpeting a terrified, "Harrrooo!"

Ranger Cron looked up and saw a large object coming down through Kefu's atmosphere heading directly for the landing area. *What is that thing?* he wondered anxiously. It wasn't a spaceship; it was coming in too fast.

It crashed down, obliterating a transporter ship and gouging a crater in the ground.

Beasts fled into the trees, and the terrified meglaphant reared up, almost trampling Ranger Cron. A machine-like alien trundled from the crater, rolling on caterpillar tracks like a tank. It had rusty-red armoured plating and an arm like a cannon. It fired a neutron blast at one of the pyramids, blowing it to pieces, then again, destroying another transporter ship and sending shrapnel flying. A piece struck the meglaphant and it trumpeted with pain. "Harrrroooo!"

The alien swung its cannon arm, preparing to fire again. "I am Tanka, and I'm here to blow this place up!"

CHAPTER ONE
THE LIFE SANCTUARY

Cosmo piloted the Dragster 7000 spaceship along Hyperway 10 between the Alpha and Delta quadrants of the galaxy. He had his helmet off, and Brain-E, the ship's bug-like brainbot, was attaching sensors to either side of his head.

"It's called the snack-o-matic, Master Cosmo," Brain-E said. "It's the latest in in-flight snack technology. All you have to do is picture a snack in your mind." Wires led from the sensors to a see-through hatch at the front of the control desk.

"OK, I'm picturing it," Cosmo replied, thinking about a Buzz Bar, his favourite chocolate bar from back on Earth. He imagined its golden wrapper, the taste of chocolate and sticky peanut butter on his tongue . . . He heard a hum from the hatch in the control desk, and looked down seeing something materializing inside. With a clang, the hatch sprang open, and he reached his hand in and retrieved it. It was a Buzz Bar, a real one! Cosmo grinned. "I could use a snack-o-matic back at home on Earth. It would save me a fortune in pocket money!"

Brain-E swiveled its bug eyes. "It should give you an energy boost for the battle ahead."

Cosmo was on the last stage of his mission, flying to Planet Kefu, home of the Galactic Life Sanctuary, to face the fifth and final invader: Tanka.

He ate a chunk from the Buzz Bar, and as he flew through the galaxy its taste brought back memories of his old life on Earth: his mum, his home, his friends. He offered a piece to his Etrusian co-pilot, Agent Nuri. "Nuri, try this. It's the most delicious chocolate bar ever."

Nuri was busy checking the spaceship's navigation console. "Thanks, Cosmo," she replied, popping the piece in her mouth. "Now get ready to exit hyperdrive."

Cosmo gripped the controls, looking out at the flashing beacons of Hyperway 10. He flicked a silver switch on the steering column and felt his ears pop as the Dragster exited hyperdrive. The craft slowed to eleven vectrons, and stars reappeared in the spacescreen. Cosmo tapped the screen, activating the star plotter, and words flashed up naming the objects in view: PLANET VISTO . . . PLANET FEX . . . PLANET KEFU . .

"Here we go," he said, flying the Dragster towards the small green planet labelled Kefu.

The Dragster flew through Kefu's atmosphere, and Cosmo looked down seeing trees below. "Is this whole place a wildlife reserve?" he asked.

"The Galactic Life Sanctuary on Planet Kefu is a multi-dimensional reserve for endangered species, Master Cosmo, with many different habitats that exist far beyond what you can see below," Brain-E replied.

"Multi-dimensional?" Cosmo asked, curious.

"That's right. Each dimension is accessed via pyramid portals built by the Kefuan rangers."

Cosmo had heard about portals before in Space Studies back at school on Earth; they were access routes into other dimensions of space-time. But he'd never dreamed he would ever get to see any.

"G-Watch scanners report that Tanka struck west of here," Nuri said. "Near the Life Sanctuary's main landing area."

Cosmo flew west, looking out for signs of the invader. "OK, Brain-E, what do we know about this alien?"

"According to G-Watch reconnaissance probes, Tanka is a metallicon evolved from discarded military hardware. He is armed with a ballistic neutron blaster and is capable of massive destruction."

As the Dragster passed above more trees, Cosmo saw a landing area cut into a swathe of forest where smoke was rising from destroyed transporter ships. A crater had been gouged into the ground, and near the landing area several ancient-looking stone pyramids had been blasted, some reduced to rubble.

"It looks like Tanka's blown the place to pieces," Nuri said.

Cosmo could make out kefuan rangers chasing after alien beasts: striped zebraves, black blubbery wartakks and even hairy ape-like plants. Cosmo circled, looking for Tanka, but could see no sign of the invader. "OK, team, I'm taking us in to land," he said.

As the Dragster touched down, he flicked a switch, opening the exit door. Cosmo stepped down to the landing area, and Nuri and Brain-E followed. It was mayhem outside. Huge transporter ships were on fire, startled creatures were running loose, and patrol buggies, hoverbikes and trailers had been destroyed or overturned.

Cosmo pushed through a herd of antogs and ducked as a fork-tailed drocox flew overhead. He splashed through a trough of disinfectant and saw a white-furred mammoth-like beast lying injured on the ground, a kefuan ranger at its side. "What happened here?" Cosmo asked him.

The ranger looked startled to see them, his scales a pale green colour.

"We're from G-Watch," Nuri said reassuringly. "We're here to help."

"A machine-like alien beamed down and started firing on us," the Kefuan explained. "I'm Ranger Cron, and this is a rare meglaphant, one of only seven left in the galaxy. It's dying."

The creature had shrapnel in its side

from an explosion and was losing blood. Its tongue had flopped out and it was panting.

Cosmo looked into its bloodshot eyes, each as wide as he was tall. "We'll save you," he said.

"I'm afraid it could be too late for that," Ranger Cron replied. "Its wounds are too large to stitch."

Nuri was looking around for Tanka, her phaser gun at the ready. "Cosmo, we must locate the invader," she said urgently.

"You find out where it went, Nuri, while I try to fix this beast," Cosmo replied. He took hold of the meglaphant's thick white fur and pulled himself up its front leg to the chunk of shrapnel in its side. "I've got an idea how we might save it."

Find out what happens in
TANKA – THE BALLISTIC BLASTER . . .

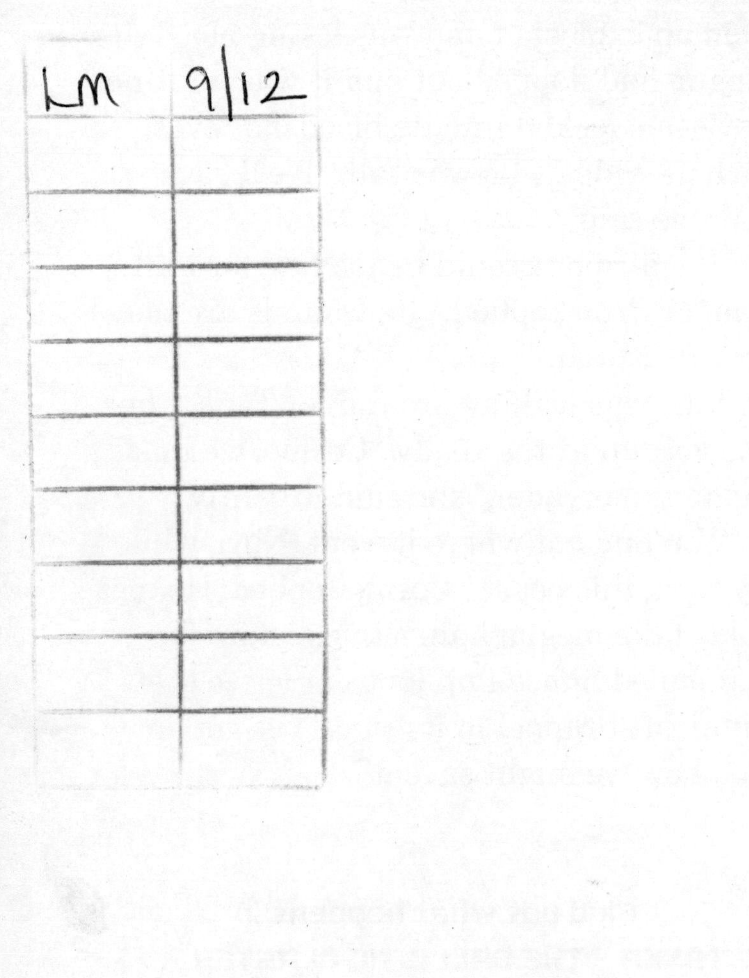
LM 9/12